Goblins Don't
Play Video Games

There are more books about the Bailey School Kids!
Have you read these adventures?

Goblins Don't Play Video Games

by Debbie Dadey
and
Marcia Thornton Jones

illustrated by John Steven Gurney

A
LITTLE APPLE
PAPERBACK

SCHOLASTIC INC.
New York   Toronto   London   Auckland   Sydney
Mexico City   New Delhi   Hong Kong

ISBN 0-439-04397-2

Text copyright © 1999 by Marcia Thornton Jones and Debra S. Dadey.
Illustrations copyright © 1999 by Scholastic Inc.
All rights reserved. Published by Scholastic Inc.
SCHOLASTIC, LITTLE APPLE PAPERBACKS, THE ADVENTURES OF THE BAILEY SCHOOL KIDS, and associated logos are trademarks of Scholastic Inc.
THE ADVENTURES OF THE BAILEY SCHOOL KIDS in design is a registered trademark of Scholastic Inc.

12 11 10 9 8 7 6 5 4 3 2 1   9/9 0 1 2 3 4/0

Printed in the U.S.A.   40

First Scholastic printing, September 1999

For Nathan, who taught me about video games, and to Alex, who can't wait to learn — DD

To Jerrie and Paul Oughton — thanks for helping me find the goblins in my stories! — MTJ

Contents

Goblins Don't
Play Video Games

1

Master Goblin

"Are you coming?" Liza asked her friend Melody. Liza held open the door to the Bailey City library, but Melody sat on the steps playing a handheld video game. Their friends Howie and Eddie waited impatiently for Melody.

Melody shook her head so hard her black pigtails slapped her on the nose. "No," she said, "you guys go in without me. I've almost got a Great Goblin cornered."

Eddie rolled his eyes. "You might be able to get all the Great Goblins, but you're never going to get the Master Goblin," he said. "I tried playing my cousin's game one time and a gargoyle zapped me before I even got to the door of the second level."

Melody paused the game and nodded knowingly. "Those flying gargoyles are pretty tough, but the Great Goblins are even worse. You never know when one will sneak up on you and what tricks they'll play."

"That's just like real goblins," Liza said. "Goblins are famous for playing pranks. They like to slam doors, knock plates off counters, and stomp across attics just to scare people."

"Then you must be a goblin," Eddie said, "because you scare me!"

Howie grinned. "There are no such things as goblins," he told Liza.

"Except in Melody's video game," Eddie added.

"And these goblins are VERY tricky," Melody said.

"I've never heard of anyone getting all the Great Goblins," Howie said. "And there's no way anyone can ever make it to the tenth level to get the Master Goblin. It's too hard."

Melody stood up from the steps and bragged, "I'm on the seventh level right now."

Eddie stared at Melody. "You're kidding. Let me see." Eddie took off his baseball cap and crowded close to Melody. Howie leaned in to see the game, too. Liza shut the door to the library and crossed her arms over her chest.

Melody played the game and the boys watched. "Get that one!" Eddie screeched and Melody zapped a gargoyle.

"Careful of that goblin," Howie said while eerie music sounded from the tiny speakers on the game.

"I wish you would turn that horrible game off," Liza snapped. "That music is creepy."

Melody looked up at Liza. "Why don't you go check out a book? I'll wait for you here. I don't really need a book right now."

"I'll stay here, too," Eddie said. "I don't ever need a book. I want to watch Melody play her Master Goblin game."

Liza frowned at Howie. "Aren't you coming?" she asked.

Howie turned red. "Okay. I guess staring at gargoyles and goblins all day is a waste of time."

"Not only that," Liza said, "I bet those little pictures are ruining your eyes." Liza sighed and went inside the library with Howie.

It was almost dark by the time Liza and Howie came outside, but Melody was still playing the game. "Aren't your fingers tired?" Liza asked Melody.

Melody shook her head. "No, but I better stop because my batteries are wearing down." Melody pushed some buttons and then shoved the game into her jacket pocket.

"Look at this great book I got," Liza said, holding up a blue book with a picture of a unicorn on the cover. "I can't wait to read it."

"I can't wait to get to level ten," Melody said as the kids started walking home.

"I'll kick the Master Goblin all over that haunted house."

The kids walked down Forest Lane and then turned left on Main Street. They were across the street from Eddie's aunt Mathilda's house. They could hear her dog, Prince Diamond, barking in the backyard.

"I wonder what's got Prince Diamond upset?" Eddie asked.

Liza pointed to the house beside Aunt Mathilda's. It was a huge old mansion that had been boarded up for years. "There's someone in there. I'm sure that's what Diamond is barking about."

The kids stared at the green glow coming from between boards in the top window of the old house. "That's strange," Eddie said. "No one has lived there in ages."

"I'll tell you what's strange," Melody said, pulling the video game out of her pocket. "That place looks just like the haunted house in my video game!"

2

Bailey Mansion

"That house is gloomy," Eddie agreed. The boards on the old mansion were gray and every shutter was either broken or missing. The windows were boarded up and the porch sagged on one end.

"Don't you know about that place?" Howie asked.

Melody shrugged. "What's to know? It's just another old house. Bailey City is full of them."

Howie shook his head. "That's the old Bailey Mansion. My mom told me to stay away from it. Everyone says it's haunted."

"They just say that to keep the kids from going inside and getting hurt on the rotten floors," Eddie said.

Liza shivered as Diamond continued

to howl. "It looks creepy to me. I wouldn't be surprised if it was haunted."

Before the kids could say another word, a moving van roared to a stop in front of the old Bailey Mansion. Diamond barked hysterically as a burly man and woman stepped out of the van and began unloading the contents.

"What kind of people move in when it's getting dark?" Liza asked.

"Who'd be nuts enough to move into Bailey Mansion to begin with?" Howie said.

"Maybe they don't know it's haunted," Melody suggested.

Eddie pointed to the unusual things the movers were unpacking. "Maybe they like it haunted," he said. The kids stared as a huge tarnished candelabra and an antique organ were unloaded. In fact, every piece of furniture they unloaded into the yard looked hundreds of years old and very fancy.

"Somebody sure likes old stuff," Eddie

said as the kids continued to stare. "Haven't they ever heard of modern conveniences?"

Howie's eyes opened wide as the movers unloaded box after box of computers and computer supplies. "They must like some modern things. Those computers are brand-new."

Liza giggled nervously. "Maybe that's so the ghosts in this house can talk over

the Internet with ghosts in haunted houses all over the world."

"Look," Melody whispered. "Maybe that's one of the ghosts now."

The kids watched as the front door to Bailey Mansion squeaked open. A short, stooped man with gray hair and a long gray beard stepped onto the rickety porch. His jeans were gray and he wore a faded gray sweatshirt. In the dim

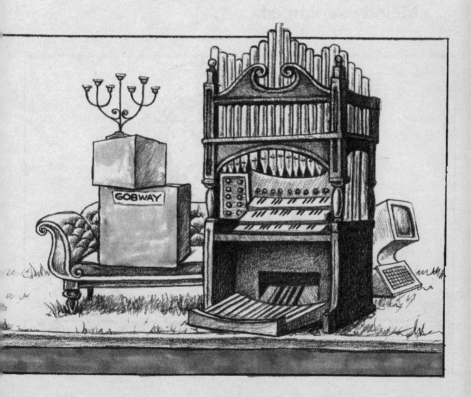

evening light, even the man's skin looked gray.

"He looks more like the Master Goblin in your Master Goblin video game," Eddie said.

Melody shuddered. "The Master Goblin is a terrible creature. We'd be in big trouble if he moved to Bailey City."

Just then, the strange man turned and stared directly at the four kids. "Hide!" Melody screamed.

3

Mr. Goble

On Monday, Liza, Eddie, and Howie met under the giant oak tree on the playground. "I had the worst nightmare last night," Liza complained. "A gray monster chased me through Bailey City Cemetery."

"I didn't get much sleep, either," Howie told her. "Somebody was playing an organ until way after midnight."

"I slept like a log," Eddie said as he stretched.

"I wonder if Melody did, too," Liza said. "She should be here by now. Maybe she's still asleep."

Howie shook his head and pointed down the street. "Melody isn't late because she slept too late. She was just too busy playing Master Goblin!"

Melody walked slowly down the sidewalk toward the playground. She was concentrating so hard on her video game that when she reached the shade of the giant oak tree she bumped right into Liza.

"You're going to walk into a tree if you don't watch where you're headed," Liza warned.

"Shhh," Melody hissed. "I'm almost to level eight. I bet I can catch the Master Goblin in no time." Just then, eerie organ music blasted from her game and a ghost popped out from a closet. "Rats." Melody sighed. "They got me."

"That music is giving me the creeps," Howie said. "It sounds just like the music that kept me up half the night."

"It's time to put that game away," Liza added. "We're going to be late for school and if Mrs. Jeepers catches you with a video game it will be much worse than losing to pretend ghosts and goblins."

The four kids were silent as they

14

thought about their third-grade teacher. Most kids were sure she was a vampire and that the brooch she always wore was full of magic. Melody slid her game into the pocket of her jacket.

"I wish we had a normal teacher," Eddie complained. "But it seems like everybody in Bailey City is strange."

"Not everyone," Melody told him. "Just the adults."

"That's not very nice to say," Liza said.

"But it's true," Eddie said as he pointed toward the front of the school. "And there's proof." His three friends looked where Eddie pointed. The little man they had seen moving into Bailey Mansion was just going through the doors.

"What is he doing here?" Howie wondered.

"I don't know," Liza said as she pulled her jacket tight. "But whatever it is, I don't think I'm going to like it."

The kids found out who the stranger was as soon as Mrs. Jeepers led them to

the computer lab. "We are so lucky," Mrs. Jeepers said in her strange Transylvanian accent. "We have a new computer teacher joining us."

Several kids cheered. Even though the computers were old and dusty, computer lab was their favorite class. Unfortunately the computer lab had been closed for at least a month because there was no teacher.

"I hope the computers still work after so much time," Melody said. "I bet they won't even turn on."

But Melody was wrong. When Mrs. Jeepers opened the door there were brand-new computers lined up in neat rows and there wasn't a speck of dust on the tables. The monitors were so clean the kids could see their own reflections.

The new teacher stood at the front of the room. It was the same little man that Howie, Liza, Melody, and Eddie had seen moving into Bailey Mansion.

"Good morning," the man said with a smile. "My name is Gordon Goble." Eddie noticed that Mr. Goble's huge teeth looked gray. They matched his gray shirt and the gray tint of his wrinkled skin.

Melody didn't notice anything because as soon as the class sat down she slipped the video game out of her pocket. She held it beneath the table and turned it on.

"What are you doing?" Liza whispered. "You're going to get in trouble."

"Shhh," Melody said. "I think I figured out how to get past that ghost." Melody continued playing as the new teacher talked to the class.

"The computer is a magnificent tool," Mr. Goble was saying. "I'm looking forward to a fun and exciting year as your computer teacher."

"The only way we'll have fun is if we get to play Master Goblin," Melody said, only she forgot to say it quietly.

Mr. Goble's smile faded. Before Liza

had time to warn Melody, the computer teacher moved across the room, heading straight for Melody. With his gnarled hand he grabbed Melody's Master Goblin video game.

4

The Great Goblin

Eerie music from the video game echoed throughout the computer lab. Melody gulped. Howie frowned. Liza whispered, "I told you so." But Eddie laughed and waited for the new teacher to send Melody to the principal's office. He was glad someone else was getting in trouble for a change.

"What is the purpose of this tiny game?" Mr. Goble asked Melody.

Melody's voice only shook a little bit when she answered. "You have to avoid the gargoyles and ghosts as you climb through the haunted house," she said. "The entire time the Great Goblins plot tricks to keep you from getting to the tenth level."

Mr. Goble scratched his chin. "What happens on the tenth level?" he asked.

"You have to catch the Master Goblin," Melody said, "before he catches you."

Mr. Goble leaned close to Melody. "What do you know about goblins?" he asked in a very low voice.

Melody scooted back before answering. "Goblins are mischievous beings that haunt houses," she said.

"They're like ghosts," a boy named Jake added.

"Goblins play tricks on people," Huey called from the next row.

"They're ugly," Eddie chipped in, "and they have warts."

Melody nodded. "And the Master Goblin is the trickiest one of all."

Mr. Goble leaned even closer to Melody until she felt his hot breath on her nose when he spoke. "And what do you know about catching goblins?" he asked, his voice barely above a whisper.

"N-n-n-othing," Melody stammered. "That's why I'm stuck on the seventh level." Melody scooted farther away from the computer teacher.

Mr. Goble nodded and examined Melody's game. Then, with a flick of his finger, Mr. Goble started a new game of Master Goblin.

The kids stared as their computer teacher tapped buttons and grinned. In no time he was up to the fifth level.

"I've never seen anybody learn that game so fast," whispered Howie.

"How did you get to be so good?" Melody blurted.

"It is easy," Mr. Goble said, "when you predict what the gargoyles and ghosts are going to do."

By the end of the class, Mr. Goble was already to the eighth level. He handed the game back to Melody as the kids filed out of the room.

"You're lucky Mr. Goble didn't tell Mrs.

Jeepers you brought your game to class," Liza told Melody.

Howie nodded. "Mr. Goble seems like a nice teacher."

"I'm not so sure," Melody said slowly. "Something about him gives me the creeps."

"Melody is just mad because he's good at her silly video game," Eddie said with a laugh. "He got to a higher level in five minutes than she was able to do all weekend. I bet our new computer teacher is going to catch the Master Goblin before Melody does!"

No sooner were the words out of Eddie's mouth than the lights flickered and went out. The kids found themselves in total darkness as an evil laugh echoed throughout the halls, sending goose bumps racing up every kid's back.

5

Scary Problems

"That was scary," Liza moaned when the lights came on and they walked into their third-grade classroom.

Eddie pointed to the chalkboard. "No," he said, "that's scary." The board was filled with at least fifty multiplication problems and their teacher was busy writing more.

The kids sat down as Mrs. Jeepers wrote still another two-digit problem. "Children," Mrs. Jeepers said, "you may begin copying the problems now."

Several kids sighed, but they took out paper to copy the problems. Melody had already written three when she heard a loud crack. Mrs. Jeepers' chalk snapped in two.

Mrs. Jeepers grabbed a fresh piece of

25

chalk from her desk and started writing. *Snap!* That chalk broke into two pieces, too.

Eddie laughed and several kids giggled. "I think somebody doesn't want us to do any more math problems," Eddie said. Mrs. Jeepers frowned and rubbed the green brooch she always wore. Instantly, the kids got quiet and Mrs. Jeepers turned to get another piece of chalk.

Just then a big crash came from the back of the room. *BAM!* A large bookcase fell over and books tumbled everywhere. The books had been messy before, but now it was much worse. Everyone stared at Eddie.

Usually whenever there was a loud noise or mess, Eddie was to blame. After all, Eddie liked to stir up trouble. But not this time. Eddie was sitting quietly at his desk, making a paper airplane.

Eddie's face turned as red as his hair. "What's everyone staring at?" he asked. "I didn't do anything."

Mrs. Jeepers frowned at the bookcase. Liza and Howie jumped up from their seats and started picking up the mess. They had just picked up three books when they heard footsteps, very loud footsteps. Only they weren't coming from the hallway. They came from the ceiling.

"How can that be?" Liza whispered to Howie. "There isn't a floor above us."

"It must be a squirrel on the roof," Howie whispered back and picked up a math book.

Stomp. Stomp. STOMP. The sound above them was very loud. "Then it must be the King Kong of all squirrels," Liza said softly.

Everyone in the classroom, even Mrs. Jeepers, stared up at the ceiling as the stomping headed toward the front of the classroom. The sound stopped right above Mrs. Jeepers.

"I'm scared," Liza whimpered.

Howie nodded. "Even Mrs. Jeepers looks worried."

Mrs. Jeepers stood at the front of the room with a broken piece of chalk in one hand. Her other hand was almost touching her brooch. She looked straight up.

Everyone in the room held their breath to see what would happen next. Liza expected more stomping, but that didn't happen. Instead, she heard knocking.

KNOCK! KNOCK! KNOCK!

Then there was silence. Liza gulped and said, "It sounds like Bailey School is haunted."

6

Goblins

"Whatever was on the roof just disappeared," Liza said after school. The kids stood under the old oak tree on the playground. The wind blew a few leaves from the tree to the ground.

"Squirrels don't disappear into thin air," Howie said.

Eddie shook his head and jumped up to swing on a tree branch. "That didn't sound like any squirrel I've ever heard. It sounded more like a rhinoceros."

"Rhinos can't disappear, either," Howie said.

Liza giggled. "I really don't think a thousand-pound rhinoceros can fit on the school roof."

Melody had been standing beside the oak tree listening to her friends. "I think

I know what was on the roof," she said suddenly.

"What was it?" Liza asked.

"Come on," Melody said. "I want to see something before I tell you." Melody led the kids down Forest Lane to Main Street.

"Why are you taking the long way home?" Eddie grumbled. "I'm hungry. I need to get a snack."

Melody glared at Eddie. "Your stomach can wait five minutes. I have to see something." When the kids turned right on Main Street Melody stopped at the corner.

"Come on," Eddie complained. "What are you stopping for? I'm starving."

Melody didn't say a word, she just pointed to the old Bailey Mansion. The kids couldn't believe their eyes. At least ten men and women were working on the outside of the old house. They had transformed it from an old run-down place into a beautiful home.

"It looks like something out of a mag-

azine," Liza said. The kids watched as one worker finished painting a corner of the house and another hammered away at a brand-new porch. Fresh white paint covered the big house and new black shutters hung at every window. Three men in green overalls planted bushes in front of the porch.

"It's like magic," Howie admitted. "I never thought that old house could look so good."

"I wish I lived there," Eddie said. "It looks like a mansion is supposed to look."

"Either that," Melody said, "or a goblin's home."

"What?" Howie, Liza, and Eddie asked together.

Melody turned to her friends and took the video game out of her jeans' pocket. "Remember the Master Goblin in my game?" she asked.

Her friends nodded. "Well," Melody continued, "I know you are going to say this is a crazy idea, but I think whatever made that noise at school has something to do with goblins."

"What are you talking about?" Eddie snapped.

Melody took a deep breath and then pulled the video game instruction booklet out of her pocket. "It's all right here," she told her friends. "The Master Goblin is the miserable spirit of a king in search of his lost kingdom. He traveled the earth searching for a land to conquer and haunt for all eternity."

Eddie nodded. "I read that in my cousin's game book. It said that the Master Goblin took over the haunted mansion in the game. It's our challenge to rid the mansion of the Master Goblin and his monster followers."

"But that's not all," Melody said, her voice barely over a whisper. "The Master Goblin is very picky about his kingdom. He makes lives miserable because he cannot stand it if a piece of paper is thrown on the floor or a bed is left unmade. The Master Goblin will not rest until the person responsible is punished!"

"The Master Goblin would definitely not be happy at my house," Eddie said with a laugh.

"What does all this goblin lore have to do with the noises we heard at school?" Howie asked.

"I think our new computer teacher," Melody said seriously, "is the Master Goblin!"

Eddie laughed. "If he's a goblin, I'll eat broccoli for breakfast."

Liza put her hand on Melody's shoulder. "Mr. Goble is just a nice old man."

Melody stomped her foot. "Mr. Goble is the Master Goblin and if we don't watch out we'll all be sorry."

7

Neat Freak

"We have to tell Principal Davis about Mr. Goble," Melody told her friends the next morning as they walked into Bailey School. "Principals like knowing when their schools are being haunted by the Master Goblin."

Liza put her hand on Melody's arm. "If you tell Principal Davis that our new computer teacher is a goblin, he'll think your brains have turned to roasted marshmallows."

"But we have to do something," Melody argued.

"The only thing I'm planning to do in the computer lab," Eddie said, "is have the time of my life."

"How can you think about having fun

when the Master Goblin is haunting our school?" Melody asked him.

"Eddie and Liza are right," Howie told Melody as they walked into their third-grade classroom. "I think that game has gone to your head."

"Wow," Liza whispered. "What happened in here?"

The four kids looked at the shelves. All the books were neatly lined up. Every desk, table, and chair had been scrubbed clean. Not a single word Eddie had written on them was left. Even the floor was spotless and shiny.

Eddie shrugged. "It looks like a neat freak had a party in our classroom."

"Either that or Mrs. Jeepers worked all night," Howie said.

But Mrs. Jeepers seemed as surprised as the kids. "What a lovely surprise," she said as soon as she walked into the room. "We must try to keep it this clean."

Eddie didn't say anything. He was too busy shredding an old math paper. He dropped the tiny pieces all over the floor. By the time they were ready for their computer class, the floor around Eddie's desk looked like it needed to be cleaned up using a rake.

"It looks like the neat freak hit the computer lab, too," Liza whispered as they filed into the computer lab.

The monitors sparkled, the windows shone, and Mr. Goble's desk was scrubbed clean. All the computers were turned on, waiting for the third-graders to start working.

"Mr. Goble likes it neat," Jake said as he passed the kids to get to his computer. "I saw him cleaning all the monitors before school. He even scrubbed the inside of the trash can."

Eddie rolled his eyes. "This guy needs a hobby. Nobody should be this clean. It isn't normal."

Mr. Goble waited until all the kids were seated. "It is a beautiful day," he said.

Melody quickly glanced out the window. Heavy gray clouds hung low over Bailey City and a chilly wind rattled the dead leaves on the tree outside the computer lab's window.

"We should celebrate such a lovely day with a treat," Mr. Goble told them. Then he whipped a big bag of chocolate bars out of his desk. The kids cheered as their new teacher handed them out.

"Mr. Goble is more than a neat freak,"

Eddie said with his mouth full of candy.

Howie nodded. "He's Mr. Nice Guy!"

Melody pushed her candy bar to the side of the table. "Be careful," she warned her friends. "Mr. Goble is being too nice."

"It's impossible to be too nice," Liza said as she started working on her computer math game.

The third-graders concentrated on their work. Everyone, that is, except Melody. She waited until Mr. Goble wasn't looking before she slipped the Master Goblin game out of her pocket. She made sure the music was turned way down, and then Melody went after the Master Goblin.

8

Level Ten

Melody was careful. When Mr. Goble headed to her side of the room to talk to Huey she paused the game and slipped it into her pocket.

Huey had raised his hand and Mr. Goble hovered over Huey's computer to help him. As soon as Huey figured out the answer, Mr. Goble reached in his pocket and pulled out a tiny toy car. "Here is a prize for working so hard," Mr. Goble told Huey.

Three more hands went up. Mr. Goble helped them all figure out their problems. Then he gave them each a prize.

Six more hands went up. Everybody wanted Mr. Goble to help them so they could get a prize, too. That gave Melody the time she needed.

She pulled the game out of her pocket and kept playing. Ghosts popped out from closets, gargoyles flew in windows, monsters reached out from under beds. Melody zapped them all.

"What are you doing?" Liza whispered. "You're going to get in big trouble."

"Shhh," Melody hissed. "I just blasted my way to level nine!"

"You're going to be blasted into Principal Davis' office if Mr. Goble sees you," Howie warned.

Eddie scooted his chair next to Melody and leaned over her shoulder so he could see. "Leave her alone. Nobody has ever gotten to level nine," he told Howie and Liza.

Melody ignored her friends and concentrated on Master Goblin. Vampires attacked from above, mummies chased her up steps, werewolves howled at the top of the stairs. Melody's fingers flew across the buttons and she got every monster that blocked her way to level ten. She

was so excited she forgot to be quiet. "I made it!" she yelled.

"Uh-oh," Eddie blurted and scooted back to his own computer.

Liza gasped. Howie pretended to be busy on his computer.

Melody glanced up from her game. Everyone else in the computer lab stared straight at her, including Mr. Goble, and he didn't look happy.

"You better put that away," Howie warned.

Melody shook her head. "I can't," she said. "Just a few more minutes and I'll have the Master Goblin. He doesn't stand a chance against me!"

Melody had barely spoken when Mr. Goble's gray eyes flashed. Suddenly, wind whipped at the tree outside the window. A branch tore loose and crashed against the window. Then, every door in Bailey Elementary slammed shut.

Several kids screamed. Eddie fell out of his chair. Howie ducked under the table. Melody was so startled, she dropped Master Goblin. Her game crashed to the floor and the screen went dead.

9

The Cure

"It's only a game," Liza said to Melody after school. The four friends were standing under the oak tree on the playground. They all stared at the blank screen on Melody's video game.

"Only a game!" Melody shrieked. "I was so close to winning. And now it's all gone. I didn't even have time to press the 'save' button."

"Accidents happen," Howie said.

"It was no accident," Melody said softly. "Mr. Goble made it happen."

"You're just lucky Mr. Goble didn't take it away from you," Howie said.

Liza nodded. "Our first-grade teacher took stuff away and didn't give it back until the end of the year."

Eddie took the game from Melody and

popped open the back. He jiggled the battery and then flipped the switch to turn it on. Instantly, the Master Goblin game appeared on the screen. "You know," Eddie said slowly, "you could do it again."

"Do what?" Melody asked.

"You could get to level ten again and beat that Master Goblin," Eddie said.

Liza groaned. "Oh, no. I was hoping you'd forget about that awful game."

Melody took the game away from Eddie and stared at the screen. She nodded. "I did it once. I could do it again."

"Now you're talking," Eddie said, patting Melody on the back. "There's nothing to stop you."

"You're wrong about that," Melody said, "as long as Mr. Goble is our teacher." She switched the game off and put it in her backpack.

"Aren't you going to play?" Eddie asked.

Melody shook her head. "First, I want to find out how to catch a real goblin."

Liza folded her arms across her chest. "Where do you intend to catch a goblin?" she asked.

Melody smiled and took off running. "The Bailey City library, of course," she yelled over her shoulder.

"There's a goblin at the library?" Eddie asked.

Howie and Liza looked at each other and shrugged. Howie raced after Melody with Eddie and Liza close behind.

The huge stone gargoyles on the roof peered down as Howie, Liza, and Eddie climbed the steps to the library. When they got inside, Melody wasn't anywhere to be found. "Where did she go?" Liza whispered.

"Maybe a goblin got her," Eddie teased.

"Something strange has been going on," Howie said. "I've never seen this place look so neat."

The kids looked around. Sure enough, every book was standing up straight without a trace of dust anywhere. Even the newspapers hung neatly on the wall rack. Nothing looked out of place, except for the backpack Eddie had just dropped on the floor.

Mr. Cooper, the librarian, rushed up to grab Eddie's backpack. "Now, children," Mr. Cooper said, "please don't make a mess. Mr. Goble has been so generous in helping us keep things neat."

"We'll be careful," Liza promised.

Mr. Cooper frowned at Eddie and handed him the backpack. Eddie sighed and put it on his back as Mr. Cooper walked away.

"All this neatness makes me nervous," Eddie said.

"Melody disappearing makes me nervous," Liza said.

Howie pointed to the stairs. "She has to be around here somewhere. Let's check the second floor."

The three kids found Melody sitting on the floor with books scattered around her. "Mr. Cooper is going to have a fit when he sees the mess you've made," Liza told Melody.

Melody giggled and looked up from a big red book. "I don't care," she said, "because I've found the cure for goblins."

10

Gerbil Food

"This is it!" Melody said early the next morning under the oak tree. She was holding up a big jar of tiny pellets. Her friends Liza, Howie, and Eddie were trying to get their yo-yos to do a trick called walk-the-dog. They grabbed their yo-yos and stared at Melody's jar.

"What's that?" Eddie asked. "Your lunch?"

Liza peered into the glass jar. "It looks like gerbil food to me."

Melody's face turned red. "Well, actually, it is gerbil food," she admitted. "But it's also the way we're going to cure our goblin problem."

"I know how to cure a goblin," Eddie said, jamming his yo-yo into his pocket.

"You give it two aspirins and call me in the morning."

"I'll call you a nincompoop if you don't stop goofing off," Melody said. "This is serious business."

Eddie snapped to attention and saluted Melody. "Sir, yes, sir. Let's knock off goblins."

Melody groaned. "We're not going to knock off anything. We're just going to persuade Mr. Goble that Bailey City is not a perfect place for goblins."

"How do we do that?" Howie asked.

Melody smiled. "I'm so glad you asked. According to the book I read, there's one thing a goblin can't stand. Messes! If a goblin sees a mess, he can't do anything else until it's cleaned up. If the mess is too much, a goblin will give up and leave to find another place to haunt."

"My grandmother can't stand messes, either," Eddie pointed out. "But that doesn't mean she's a goblin."

Howie nodded. "Most teachers like it neat, too."

"Eddie and Howie are right," Liza said. "For all we know, Mr. Goble is just a nice computer teacher who doesn't like messes. After all, I'm pretty sure goblins don't play video games."

"Besides," Eddie said, "who cares if Mr. Goble is the Master Goblin? He gives out candy and prizes. I think he's nice."

"That's just more proof that Mr. Goble is a goblin. My book said goblins give treats to boys and girls when they're good. But if they're not good—watch out! And if Mr. Goble really is the Master Goblin," Melody said, her voice dropping to a whisper, "then he won't stop until Bailey City is spotless. And he'll make it stay spotless. Are you prepared to live in a town where not a single toy can be left on the floor, not a crumb of food can be dropped to the ground, and not a speck of dirt can be found?"

Eddie shivered. "That does sound terrible," he said. "But we don't know for sure that Mr. Goble is a goblin."

"We can use this gerbil food to find out," Melody explained. "All we have to do is sprinkle it over the computer lab floor."

Liza gasped. "That's mean. After all, Mr. Goble just cleaned the computer lab."

"I know," she said. "But if he's really a goblin, he'll clean it up right away. According to my research, farmers from long ago found out the way to get rid of a goblin is by throwing tiny flaxseeds on the floor. A goblin will stop to pick them up since he can't stand messes. After a while, he'll get tired of picking up seeds and fly off to find a better place to haunt."

Liza pointed to the jar Melody held. "But those aren't seeds."

Melody shrugged. "I don't even know what flaxseeds look like, but I thought gerbil food would be tiny enough."

"What if Mr. Goble isn't really a goblin?" Howie asked.

"Then the mess will still be there when we come in and we'll sweep it up," Melody told her friends.

Eddie fell to the ground and pretended to choke. "We have to clean up a mess?" he said. "That would really kill me."

"Very funny," Melody said, "but we have to hurry before Mr. Goble gets here."

Howie nodded. "I guess it's the only way to find out for sure."

The four kids quietly slipped inside the school building. Their shoes made squeaks on the tile floor as they eased into the computer room.

Melody poured the little pellets into everyone's hands and then the kids scattered them onto the floor. Liza dropped a little around the trash can and door. Howie scattered his around Mr. Goble's desk. Melody put hers under the computer desks. Eddie stood in the center of the room and threw his straight up in the

air. Most of his pellets landed in his hair. "Look," Eddie said with a laugh. "I'm a gerbil treat."

"Be careful," Melody warned. "We don't want any pellets to get on the computers."

"Shhh," Liza hissed, pointing to the doorknob. "Someone's coming." The four kids stared as the doorknob slowly turned.

11

Goblin Goulash

"We're goblin goulash," Liza whimpered.

"Only if he finds us," Eddie said as he scrambled under a table. Liza, Howie, and Melody followed him. They huddled together as the door slowly creaked open.

Crunch. Crunch. CRUNCH. Gerbil food crumbled under big gray shoes as somebody walked across the computer lab. Suddenly the footsteps stopped.

"Ohhhhh! Ohhhhh! OHHHHHH!" whoever was in the room moaned. Then he turned and rushed into the hall.

"He sure didn't like the sound of crunching gerbil food," Howie said.

Liza shivered. "It upset him so much he moaned just like a ghost," she said.

"Or a goblin," Melody added. "We have to get out of here before Mr. Goble comes back."

"We don't know for sure that it was Mr. Goble," Howie said as he crawled out from under the table.

"Who else would be brave enough to come into a goblin's room?" Melody asked.

"A detective looking for your brains," Eddie told Melody as he stood up.

Liza patted Melody on the shoulder. "Eddie's right. This whole thing is silly. Let's forget this goblin game and get to our classroom before Mrs. Jeepers finds out what we've done."

"This is no game," Melody warned her friends as the four kids sneaked out of the computer lab. But Eddie, Liza, and Howie were in too much of a hurry to listen.

Eddie led the way. He rushed down the hallway and turned a corner. When he did, he crashed right into Mr. Goble.

Howie bumped into Eddie. Liza and Melody ran into Howie. They all landed in a pile in the middle of the hall. Books slid out of backpacks, and paper flew everywhere.

"We're sorry," Liza said as Mr. Goble helped untangle the mess of legs and arms. "We didn't mean to run into you."

Melody and Howie quickly gathered their books and papers.

"We didn't know you were there," Eddie blurted. Eddie hopped up from the floor and wiped off the seat of his pants. When he did, gerbil food plopped to the floor around his sneakers.

Melody gasped as Mr. Goble reached out and plucked a gerbil pellet from Eddie's hair. "Do you always keep animal food hidden in your hair?" Mr. Goble asked.

Eddie backed away from Mr. Goble. "N-n-no," Eddie stammered. "I — I was doing a science experiment this morning to see if gerbils could sniff out food."

Just then, the bell rang. "We have to go," Liza said as politely as she could. And then the four kids hurried down the hall.

"We're doomed," Melody said when they stopped outside their third-grade classroom. "Mr. Goble knows we were the ones who put the gerbil food all over his room."

"We're not in trouble," Howie said. "Eddie is."

"That's right," Liza said with a little clap. "Eddie is the only one he caught with the pellets."

"I'm not worried," Eddie said. He stood up tall and puffed out his chest. "Mr. Goble thinks I was doing a science experiment. Thanks to my quick thinking, I have nothing to worry about."

But Eddie was wrong. Very wrong.

12

Goblin's Playground

The four kids hurried to their desks. Melody, Liza, and Howie pulled out paper and pencils and started copying the spelling sentences Mrs. Jeepers had on the board. Eddie pulled paper from his desk, too. When he did, sparkly pink, blue, and yellow Superballs hit the floor and bounced wildly down the aisle. They rolled to a stop right beside Mrs. Jeepers' pointy black shoes.

Jake and Huey laughed. Melody and Liza gasped. Howie hid behind his spelling book. Everybody stared at Eddie. Including Mrs. Jeepers.

Eddie's face turned as red as his hair. "Those aren't mine," he blurted.

Mrs. Jeepers did not look convinced.

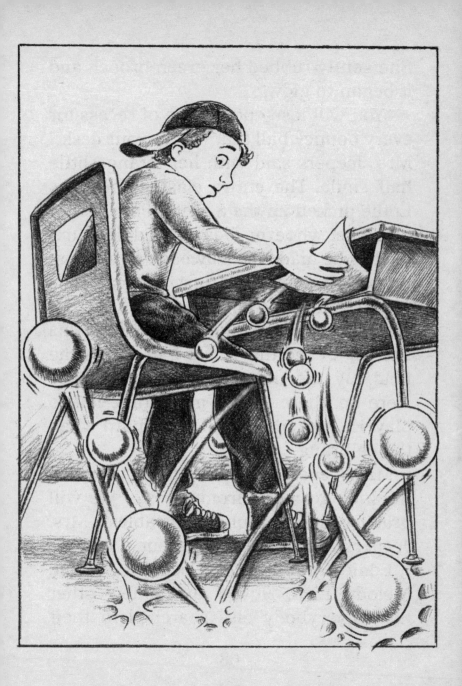

She gently rubbed her green brooch and it began to glow.

"You will lose one minute of recess for every bouncy ball that was in your desk," Mrs. Jeepers said with her strange little half smile. The entire class counted as Eddie picked up the Superballs.

"I'll get whoever did this," Eddie mumbled as he made his way back to his seat. "Those thirteen balls just cost me thirteen minutes of fun."

During recess, Eddie watched as his friends kicked the soccer ball across the field. By the time his thirteen minutes were up, there wasn't much time left to play. He kicked the ball extra hard when the bell rang.

Mrs. Jeepers was ready for math when the kids got back from recess. "We will practice the multiplication tables," Mrs. Jeepers said. "Please take out a pencil."

Eddie grabbed his pencil. So did Melody, Liza, Howie, and a few other kids. Everybody else searched in their pencil boxes, under books, and inside notebooks.

"I can't find my pencil," Carey finally said.

"Somebody took my pencil," Huey called out.

"Mine's missing, too," Jake added.

Mrs. Jeepers' eyes flashed and she looked straight at Eddie. "I didn't take their pencils," Eddie said.

"Please empty your desk to be sure," Mrs. Jeepers said in a very quiet voice.

Eddie reached in his desk and pulled out a wad of crumpled papers. As soon as he did, a bundle of pencils spilled on the floor.

"Eddie took our pencils!" Carey yelled out.

"I did not," Eddie said. "I mean, I have them, but I didn't take them."

Mrs. Jeepers did not look like she believed Eddie. "You must complete an extra math problem for every pencil found in your desk," she said in her strange Transylvanian accent. "Please return the pencils."

Everybody counted as Eddie hurried to give the pencils to their owners. Then he slid back into his desk and started on the extra thirteen math problems. He barely had time to finish before computer class.

Mr. Goble smiled as the kids filed into the sparkling-clean computer lab. Not a trace of gerbil food remained anywhere. "The computer is a wonderful writing tool," he told the third-graders. "Today you can spend the entire time writing stories, poems, or maybe even apology letters." When he said apology letters, Mr. Goble looked at Eddie and grinned.

Eddie didn't notice. He started a story about a character named Super Eddie who got back at a bully. He was having so much fun he had to hurry when Mr. Goble told them to print their work.

Mr. Goble handed each student their printed pages as they left the room. When he did a few girls gasped. A cou-

ple more girls read their papers and looked up at Eddie. Carey batted her eyelashes at Eddie and a girl named Helen turned red and giggled.

Then Mr. Goble handed Liza and Melody a printout. They didn't look at them until they were in the hallway. When they did, Liza gasped and Melody groaned.

"What have you done?" Liza asked, shoving her paper under Eddie's nose.

Eddie read the words. His face turned a sickly shade of green and his knees started shaking. Then he read them again. His lips moved as he said the words to himself.

"What does it say?" Howie asked and snatched the paper from Eddie. He read out loud, "'Violets are blue. Daffodils are yellow. I'm stuck on you like glue. Can I be your fellow?'"

"Look," Melody said, pointing to the bottom of the paper. "It's signed '*SWAK: SENT WITH A KISS.*'"

"And Eddie's name is typed at the end," Liza added.

"AAARRRRGGHH!" Eddie yelled. "I'm doomed."

"Don't be silly," Liza said. "It's just a love note, not the end of the world."

Eddie slid down the wall until he was sitting on the floor. "Love notes ARE the end of the world," he moaned. "I can't believe somebody gave these horrible notes to all the girls."

"Not all the girls," Melody said slowly. "Just thirteen of us."

"How do you know?" Liza asked.

"First there were thirteen Superballs," Melody explained, "thirteen missing pencils, and now there are thirteen love letters from Eddie."

"They are NOT from me!" Eddie nearly yelled. "Wait until I get my hands on the dirty culprit who did this to me!"

"You have to catch him first," Melody said. "And I know for a fact that catching him is close to impossible."

"What are you talking about?" Eddie snapped.

"I'm talking about catching the Master Goblin," Melody told him. "Mr. Goble has turned our school into a goblin's playground because he knows you scattered gerbil pellets all over the computer lab. I wonder what other pranks he has planned for you."

Eddie stood up from the floor and put his hands on Melody's shoulders. "Tell me what to do to get rid of this goblin curse," he said. "Whatever it is, I'll do it!"

13

Heavy Artillery

"We have to make a mess," Melody told her friends as they walked down the hall toward their classroom.

Liza shook her head. "We already tried that. Mr. Goble cleaned it up faster than Eddie can burp."

Eddie burped just to prove the point and Melody frowned. "No," Melody said. "That was just the beginning. We have to bring out the heavy artillery."

"That sounds like war," Howie said.

"Now you get it," Melody agreed. "Here's what we have to do." Melody whispered her plan while Eddie grinned and Liza gasped.

Howie swallowed hard and said, "If Mrs. Jeepers or Principal Davis found

out we did something like that, they'd make us stay after school for the rest of our lives."

"That's right," Liza said. "We'll be in a nursing home and still have to come here after school."

"You guys worry too much," Melody said. "Just bring the stuff to school tomorrow and I'll take care of the rest."

The next morning the kids came early with backpacks and plastic bags stuffed with white foam packing peanuts, rice cereal, and three huge bags of cheese popcorn. Quietly the kids slipped inside the school and to the computer room. The room was pitch-black, except for the whirring of one computer.

"Let's do it," Melody said firmly.

"I don't know if this is such a good idea," Liza whispered. "What if Mr. Goble isn't a goblin?"

Eddie ripped open a bag of cheese popcorn. "He's a goblin, all right. How else could he have played all those tricks on me?"

"Eddie has a point," Howie said. "What if Mr. Goble starts playing tricks on everybody?"

"I think our mess will work this time," Melody said. She pulled her small video game out of her pocket. "I got all the way to level ten last night and beat the Master Goblin."

"Holy Toledo!" Eddie said in amazement. "I can't believe you did it."

Melody nodded. "I got rid of that goblin, and now I'm getting rid of the one at Bailey School." She tossed a huge handful of packing peanuts on the floor. The rest of the kids got busy and soon the floor was ankle deep in peanuts, popcorn, and rice cereal.

Eddie threw a handful into the air. "It's snowing! It's snowing!" he said with a laugh.

Liza gulped when she saw the huge

mess they'd made. "I hope we did the right thing," she said.

"We did," Melody assured her. "But we'd better get out of here before Mr. Goble catches us."

The kids hurried out of the classroom and shut the door carefully behind them. Then they ran smack into their teacher, Mrs. Jeepers.

"Hello, children," Mrs. Jeepers said, touching her hand to the green brooch she always wore. "What are you doing here so early in the day?"

Howie's face turned bright red. "We were looking for Mr. Goble," Howie explained.

"Haven't you heard?" Mrs. Jeepers asked. "Mr. Goble got another job, working at the Internal Revenue Service. His last day was yesterday."

Eddie, Melody, Howie, and Liza stood in the hallway with their mouths hanging wide open as Mrs. Jeepers clicked down the hall. Finally, Eddie turned to Melody. "You mean we made that huge mess for nothing?"

"It wasn't for nothing. We did it to get rid of a goblin," Melody said, "only the goblin was smarter than we were."

"Nobody is smarter than me," Eddie said proudly.

Melody shook her head. "You're wrong, Eddie," she said. "Mr. Goble played one last trick on us, and it was the worst trick of all because now we have to clean up the mess we made before anybody else finds it."

Eddie opened the computer room door and stared at the mounds of cheese popcorn, packing peanuts, and rice cereal. All four kids groaned.

"Mr. Goble must've been the Master Goblin to come up with a mean trick like this," Howie said as he started throwing rice cereal into the trash can.

"Or maybe Mr. Goble was never a gob-

lin to begin with," Liza suggested. "After all, we're the ones who made the mess."

"And it's all Melody's fault," Eddie grumbled as he stuffed packing peanuts into Howie's book bag.

Howie nodded and grabbed a handful of cheese popcorn. He threw it at Melody and said, "After all, goblins don't play video games!"

Debbie Dadey and Marcia Thornton Jones have fun writing stories together. When they both worked at an elementary school in Lexington, Kentucky, Debbie was the school librarian and Marcia was a teacher. During their lunch break in the school cafeteria, they came up with the idea of the Bailey School kids.

Recently Debbie and her family moved to Aurora, Illinois. Marcia and her husband still live in Kentucky where she continues to teach. How do these authors still write together? They talk on the phone and use computers and fax machines!

Creepy, weird, wacky, and funny things happen to the Bailey School Kids!™ Collect and read them all!

The Adventures of THE BAILEY SCHOOL KIDS®

Available wherever you buy books, or use this order form

Scholastic Inc., P.O. Box 7502, Jefferson City, MO 65102

Please send me the books I have checked above. I am enclosing $_____ (please add $2.00 to cover shipping and handling). Send check or money order — no cash or C.O.D.s please.

Name _____

Address _____

City _____ State/Zip _____

Please allow four to six weeks for delivery. Offer good in the U.S. only. Sorry, mail orders are not available to residents of Canada. Prices subject to change.   BSK1098